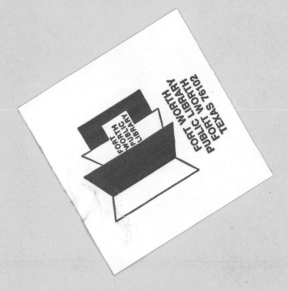

TIDDALICK THE FROG

Books by Susan Nunes

COYOTE DREAMS

TIDDALICK THE FROG

For Mother and Dad   —S. N.

To Mi Le   —J.H. C.

TIDDALICK THE FROG

Susan Nunes

illustrated by Ju-Hong Chen

Atheneum   1989   New York

Long ago in the Dreamtime, long before people roamed the earth, there lived a gigantic frog named Tiddalick. Tiddalick was so big that his shadow turned day into night, so powerful that his voice drowned the thunder, so heavy that a single hop shook the ground for miles and miles around.

One morning Tiddalick awoke with an enormous thirst, and this enormous thirst put him in a very ill humor. Grumbling loudly to himself, he lumbered down to the river, knocking down trees and scattering everything in his path. When he reached the water's edge, he took a deep breath, plunged his great head into the water, and began to drink.

All day and all night Tiddalick drank. When the sun rose, Tiddalick the Frog sat like a mountain beside the dry riverbed. In his tremendous stomach was all the fresh water of the world.

Day after day he sat, motionless and full. Cracks appeared in the dry earth. Soil turned to sand. Dust was everywhere. Without water, every green and growing thing withered and died. The world had become a desert.

Still Tiddalick sat, swollen with his precious load. Without water, creatures everywhere began to sicken and die. One by one the animals went to Tiddalick to tell him their troubles.

"There is nowhere to escape the heat," said Kangaroo, shaking the sand out of her pouch.

"My milk has dried up," said Numbat, "and my little ones are so weak they cannot hold on to me."

"So weak," echoed her babies.

Koala Bear said shyly, "All the eucalyptus leaves are gone." He held up a dead branch and shook his head.

And Bandicoot, too tired to speak, tucked his muzzle between his front legs, folded his long, furry ears over his eyes, and fell asleep.

But even in the face of this misery, Tiddalick did nothing but roll his big eyes and shift his monstrous body.

"What should we do?" asked the Dingoes.

"Perhaps we should beg and plead," said Quokka. He held up his paws, brought his tail between his hind legs, and sat on it.

No, no. Everyone knew that would do no good.

"Perhaps we should *insist!*" said Emu, ruffling her feathers.

"Perhaps we should *force* him to return the water," said Kangaroo. She stamped her big feet and thumped her heavy tail.

But when Tiddalick's shadow fell on them, their courage fled like dry leaves before the wind.

"We're doomed," they agreed sadly.

Then wise old Wombat twitched his hairy nose and said, "If we can make Tiddalick *laugh*, he will forget his ill humor and let the water go."

All the creatures gathered near Tiddalick. First, Kookaburra told his best funny stories, laughing crazily at his own jokes. But Tiddalick did not laugh. All he did was blink once or twice.

Next, Emu and Kangaroo tried to outjump each other. They jumped and jumped until they collapsed in a pile of legs and feathers. But Tiddalick only shifted his huge bulk and growled in boredom.

All through the day, the animals of the world tried to make the great frog laugh. Lizard furled and unfurled his magnificent frill. Cuscus counted her spots and crossed her yellow eyes. And Bandicoot tied his ears together. Still, Tiddalick only sat. And sat.

Finally, even Wombat shook his wise old head.

"We're doomed," the animals moaned.

Then, suddenly, there was a tiny cry. "Wait for me!" It was little Noyang, the eel, squirming his way out of the hardened mud of the riverbank.

"It's only Noyang," said Quokka. "What can he do that we haven't done?" He pulled his tail between his hind legs and sat on it again.

"Yes," echoed the Dingoes, "what can he do?"

"He can try," said Wombat.

"He can try!" snickered Kookaburra, hopping about in a fit of laughter.

Noyang slithered up to Tiddalick. Balancing on the tip of his tail, he looked up at the great frog. Tiddalick glowered down at him.

Noyang bowed forward until his head touched Tiddalick's huge feet. Next, he bowed backward until his head brushed the ground behind him. Then he began to dance.

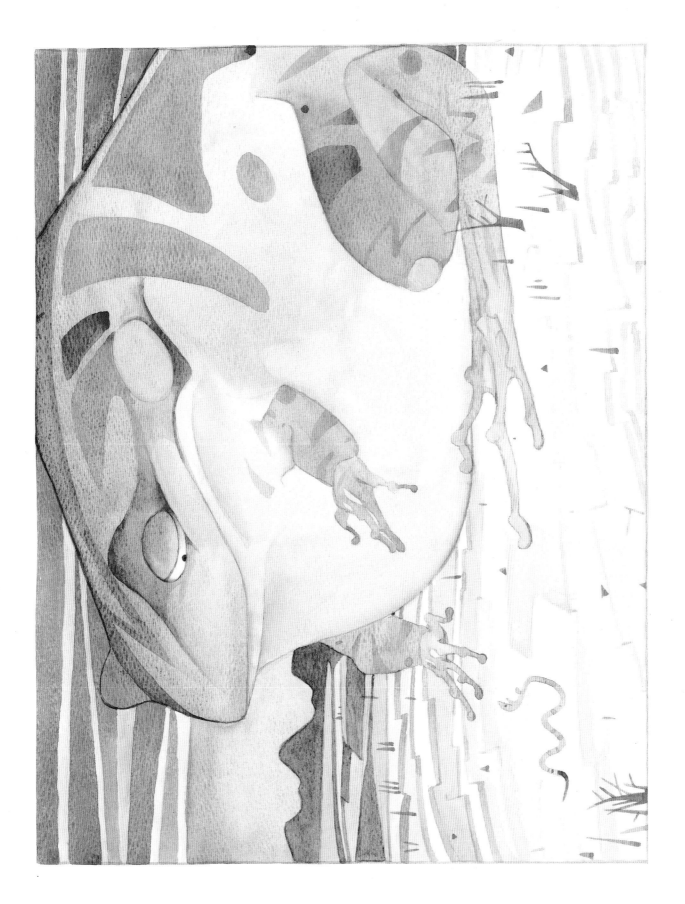

At first, his movements were slow and graceful, like ripples on a pond or waves of grass in the wind. But soon Noyang quickened his pace.

He coiled and uncoiled his slippery little body. He twisted and turned...whirled and twirled. He shimmied and shook...squiggled and squirmed. He wriggled and jiggled. He flounced and bounced. He flipped and flopped. He bumped and whomped. He did spirals, curlicues, corkscrews. Hoops, loops, and...ARABESQUES!

Tiddalick's eyes began to twinkle.

Noyang crawled upon Tiddalick's feet, danced onto his legs, then snaked his way onto the frog's swollen stomach. There he did his wildest movements.

Tiddalick's cheeks began to tremble.

The animals laughed. They laughed until they forgot their thirst. They laughed until they forgot their hunger. They laughed until they forgot Tiddalick. There was only little Noyang's wonderful dance.

Tiddalick peered at the commotion on his swollen belly, and his sides began to shake.

But suddenly Noyang slipped. To save his dance, he looped himself into a wheel, which wobbled off Tiddalick's stomach and plunged to the ground. When the dust settled, Noyang was tied in a double knot!

"Help!" he cried.

The animals rushed to untie him, but he was stuck fast.

"THIS IS NOT FUNNY!" groaned Noyang.

Then something happened. Tiddalick laughed.

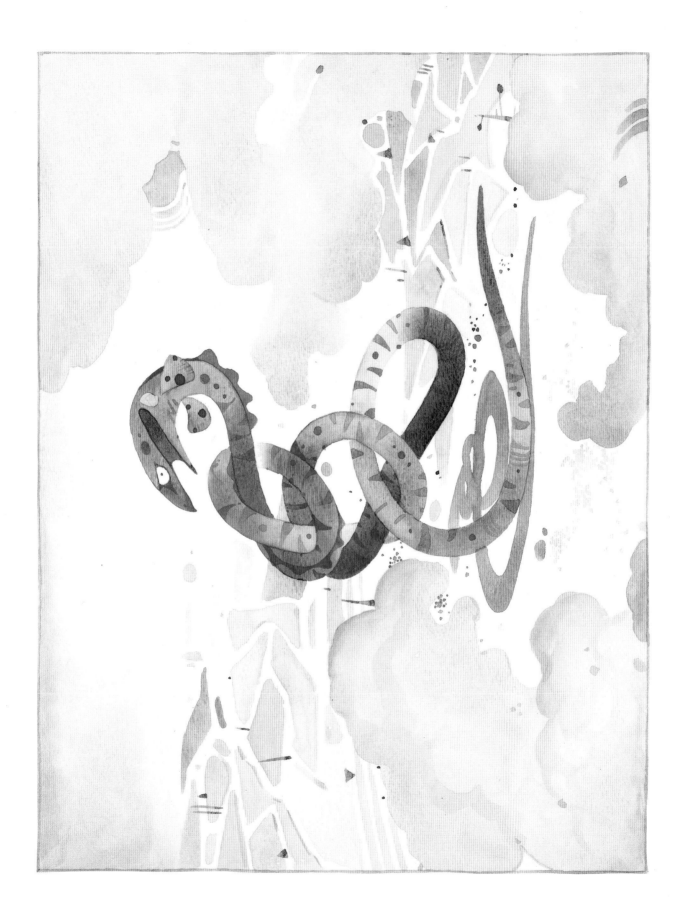

At first it was just a low rumble that began deep in the great frog's belly and only raised a few dust clouds. But it grew and grew until the heavens thundered and the earth shook and all the animals ran for cover.

How Tiddalick laughed! He laughed so long that he forgot his ill humor, and he laughed so hard that the waters GUSHED from his mouth to nourish the earth once again.

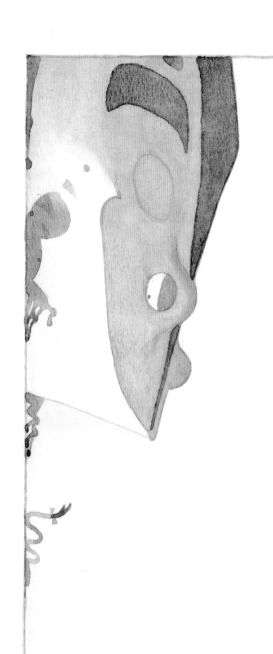

And, yes, once little Noyang untied himself, he stayed close to Tiddalick's side, just to be sure the giant frog never woke in an ill humor again.

Atheneum

Macmillan Publishing Company
866 Third Avenue, New York, NY 10022
Collier Macmillan Canada, Inc.
First Edition   Designed by Eliza Green
Printed in Hong Kong

1 2 3 4 5 6 7 8 9 10

Library of Congress Cataloging-in-Publication Data
Nunes, Susan.
Tiddalick the frog/Susan Nunes; illustrated by Ju-Hong Chen.
—1st ed.   p.   cm.
Summary: Retells the Aboriginal tale about what happened when the
giant frog Tiddalick had such a great thirst that he drank all the
fresh water of the world.
ISBN 0-689-31502-3
[1. Australian aborigines—Legends.]   I. Chen, Ju-Hong, ill.   II.Title.
PZ8.1.N797   1989   398.2'452789'0899915—dc 19   [E]   89-1   CIP
AC